Muscle Girl Collection

VOL I

By
Ash Max

Amelia: Muscle Girl Tales I

Chapter 1.

Danny sighed as he stood at the entrance to the gym. This was probably a stupid idea, he reflected. Hadn't he tried to get buff before? And look where that got him. He was just as weak and weedy as he had always been. Somehow he had been talked into signing up for a six month membership, though, and he was damned if he was going to pay all that money for nothing. The girl who had been recruiting new members was very attractive, and her shirt was very low cut. He hadn't wanted to look pathetic in front of her and confess that the gym was intimidating to him, and he had boldly signed up for six months, thinking it would impress her.

Idiot, he chided himself. She worked at a gym! She was surrounded by guys who worked out every single day. He wasn't anything special – in fact, he thought bitterly, he was probably special only because of how tiny he was. Danny was kind of sensitive about this, he would admit. His last girlfriend had left him a few months back and the rejection still stung. He'd seen her out in town the other week with whoever her new boyfriend was and the guy was enormous. Danny wasn't stupid, he knew he wasn't going to win her back or anything, but he had to admit. The idea of at least not looking so pathetic the next time they bumped into each other was appealing. Maybe next time he wouldn't feel the need to hide behind a shrub. He swung his gym bag back and forth between his hands, stalling for time. He was supposed to have a personal trainer session – it was one of the perks of signing up. Four free sessions with one of their trainers.

Danny wasn't looking forward to it. It would probably be some enormous meathead, he thought, some guy whose arms were thicker than his waist. Some guy who looked like his ex's new boyfriend. Danny always hated guys like that, the way they walked around like they owned the place. He frowned, and looked at his watch. He needed to head in, or he'd be late. He tried to pull back his shoulders and felt something ping in his neck as he did. Maybe there could be some benefits to joining a gym, actually. He was trying to think positive.

He walked up to the front desk, trying to ignore the fact everyone here looked like they could bench him, or maybe snap him in half. "I'm here to see uh…" his mind went blank. "One of your trainers? I'm Danny" he added. The girl behind the desk was wearing a tiny pair of gym shorts and a sports bra. It was very distracting. Maybe a meathead trainer would be preferable to embarrassing himself in front of a hot girl, he thought.
"We've got you with Amelia" she said brightly, looking up and smiling.

Danny's heart sank. "Oh. Great" he said, trying to sound enthusiastic and failing miserably.
"She's right over there" continued the girl, blithely unaware of how Danny's heart was sinking into his shoes at the idea of a female personal trainer seeing how weak he was. She pointed over Danny's shoulder and he turned

around, seeing a spectacularly built woman standing by the lockers, who gave a quick wave and smiled. There was no turning back now. He couldn't get out of this one, he realized. "Thanks" he muttered, before turning to go and greet Amelia.

"So you're Danny?" she said.

"Yep" said Danny, feeling stupid already. "I'm um… I haven't been here before" he said, trying to sound confident.

Amelia smirked. "I could have guessed that" she said, her eyes quickly scanning over his body in a way that made him feel virtually naked. He'd heard the phrase 'undressing with her eyes' before, but he had always assumed it wouldn't feel quite so… exposing. He looked back, figuring it was fair game to size her up as well. She was bound with tight thick muscles, her arms hard and tanned, her biceps bulging out from underneath the tight t-shirt she wore. Thick slabs of muscle gave her torso a V-shape, her waist slender and defined, and her shoulders were capped, the delts prominent even under her clothes. As she moved, the sinew of her arms did too, and he noticed her forearms were jacked too – thick veins sticking out as she moved, every gesture seeming to flex and tense her muscles. She smirked as she noticed him staring.

"A few months… well. Maybe a year or two and you might have muscles like this" she said. "Come on, let's get started. Let's see if you can put in the hard work." She turned on her heel and started off swiftly towards the weight room. Danny jammed his bag in a locker and headed after her, trying not to do anything too embarrassing like breaking into a trot.

Within maybe 10 minutes he was panting and worried his chest was going to explode. Or implode. He wasn't sure. He didn't feel very good. "I don't feel very good" he said out loud.

Amelia looked at him with an expression of disdain on her face. "You don't look very good either" she said. Danny was too exhausted to protest that he was the paying customer here. "Come on, you can get five more reps, I know you can" she said. He wasn't sure if she was trying to sound bossy or encouraging. Maybe it didn't matter. There was clearly no arguing with her. Grunting, he heaved the barbell up again and weakly swung it in an arc, squeezing out one more bicep curl. "Four to go" said Amelia, an evil grin on her face.

Danny gritted his teeth and felt like his arms were burning, as though acid was running through his veins. He closed his eyes tightly and focused on trying to lift the weight one more time.

Chapter 2.

The rest of the training session passed in much the same way. Amelia seemed to delight in humiliating him. When she demonstrated how to perform a lift she would make it look effortless, the weights flying gracefully through the hair, and hardly breaking a sweat. Her muscles tensed and flexed, their strength and power obvious to behold. Danny wasn't sure if he was envious or turned on or furious.

"I'll just take a few plates off before you try" she said. "Maybe all of them. I think just the empty bar is probably enough for you."

Danny wanted to protest but he had almost toppled over trying to press it above his head ten minutes ago, so he suspected he didn't really have a leg to stand on here. Surely the hour must be almost up. This felt like torture.

Mercifully, Amelia seemed to have the same thought. She glanced at her watch. "Well! That's almost us for the day" she said cheerfully. "Good work today, I'll see you again on Thursday." Her whole demeanour shifted, as though she had just been inhabiting the role of a cruel and dominant demon, forcing him through set after set.

"Thanks" said Danny, looking around for somewhere to sit down. He needed to shower but he also felt like his legs might be about to give out under him.

"Do a quick warm down on the treadmill" said Amelia, absently. "Twenty minutes or so should do it."

Danny nodded. He was not going anywhere near a

treadmill, he decided. He felt exhausted and he also couldn't figure out how he felt about Amelia. He hated her, obviously. But also, something about the way she had been teasing and humiliating him was… he shook his head. All the exertion must be doing something funny to his brain, he decided. There was no way he was enjoying this. It was probably just that it was the first time a woman had paid any real attention to him in months, he decided. That was it. Nothing more complicated than that. He watched Amelia go, her tight ass barely covered by the thin lycra of her shorts. That was probably the other reason he was feeling like this, he thought. She was objectively hot. She just also happened to look like she could probably snap him like a twig if she wanted to.

The next session, on Thursday, passed roughly the same way. Danny had barely started to recover from the first session, and his muscles felt like they'd been run through a mincer. He couldn't believe she expected him to lift even more than last time. "No pain no gain" she said sweetly. Danny groaned. "Unless you feel like quitting" she said, her voice dropping to a low and husky whisper. He felt a surge of heat run through his cheeks that had nothing to do with the exertion he was subjecting his body to. There were no two ways around it. Something about how Amelia was teasing him was turning him on. He wondered how long he had had this latent fetish for. Had muscular women always done it for him? His train of thought was interrupted by the screaming pain in his pecs.

"One more set" said Amelia, decisively. Danny was lying on a bench, sweating heavily. Amelia was standing by his side, and he was trying to work out where to look. Her muscular thighs were level with his head and the tiny outfit she was wearing left very little to the imagination. He didn't know what was polite, and staring at any part of her seemed rude. He suspected he didn't want to piss her off.

"One more?" he asked.

Amelia nodded. "I'll spot you" she said, moving to stand just above his head. Danny continued trying not to look at her, afraid that if he did his body might betray him. He was so exhausted he would honestly be surprised if his cock could get hard, but he didn't want to tempt fate. "On three" said Amelia, and Danny nodded. He looked straight ahead, at the bar, reaching up and grasping it firmly, trying not to notice how tiny his arms looked next to Amelia's. Her forearms were thicker than his biceps, he realized.

He pressed out a rep before realizing he was so close to her he could smell her sweat. He could smell her pussy. He tried to put the thought out of his head and instead focus on not dropping the barbell on his chest but it was hard not to focus on it now he had realized. *She smells so good…* he thought, and gritted his teeth, trying to force the barbell upwards.

"Up!" barked Amelia, her hands darting out to hover even closer to the bar. Danny pushed in vain, his muscles filled with a searing tension, before she grabbed the bar and lifted it back into place as though it weighed nothing at all. "I think that's all for today, huh?" she said. Her eyes slid over his body and he realized with a dawning horror that he was hard after all. "Looks like you enjoyed the workout today" she said with a grin, before turning to leave. Danny wanted to sink through the floor.

Chapter 3.

Danny's phone beeped while he was at lunch. He glanced at the screen, his heartrate suddenly quickening when he saw it was from Amelia.

Can we change our time tomorrow? said the message.

Sure sent back Danny.

Great. 8pm ok by you? I had a new program in mind and the gym should be quieter then.

Sounds great he sent in reply, with an enthusiasm he didn't remotely feel.

When he arrived at the gym the following night, it was almost empty. Honestly, he was surprised by how much it had emptied out, but he figured most people came in straight after work then headed home. "Looks like we've got it almost all to ourselves" came a voice from behind him, making him jump. Amelia was dressed as she usually was, in tight and tiny shorts, and a sports bra. She was wearing a tank top today, which pulled tight across her chest, highlighting her pecs. Danny wondered if he would ever be even half as muscular as she was. "Follow me" she said, and Danny obediently trudged towards the weight room.

Amelia took him through several more lifts, different to what they had done the past couple of sessions. Her body was pressed up against his as she demonstrated, the muscle of her chest pressed against his back, and he could feel how hard she was, her entire body built and pumped.

It reminded him of how weak he was, and he wondered idly if she would be able to push him around if she tried. He attempted to get rid of that thought. It was embarrassing enough that she had seen him getting hard the other day, he didn't need a repeat of that performance.

"Something on your mind?" she asked, her voice in his ear as she stood behind him.

Danny shook his head. "Just trying to focus on moving my hips properly" he lied.

Amelia placed her hands on his hips, tugging him into position, then back into her body. "Just like this" she said. Danny shivered at the feeling of being pulled around by her. He could feel her strength, even in the subtle gesture. He felt rather than heard a giggle run through her body. "Do you like that?" she asked, not moving her hands from his hips. There was no one around them.

"Maybe" said Danny. Then, "yes" he admitted.

"I thought so" she said, and he could hear the smile, the triumph, in her voice. "You like how much stronger I am, huh?" Danny nodded, hot waves of shame and arousal flooding through his body. Amelia's hands slid from his hips down to his shorts, one grabbing his hard cock through his shorts. "You like it a lot, don't you" she whispered. "You like knowing I could pick you up if I wanted to, don't you? Feeling my strength, feeling my hard body pressed up next to yours, all my muscles flexing." Danny had his eyes shut tightly, his breath coming in short pants.

Amelia spun him around so he was facing her, and shoved down his gym shorts, grabbing his cock and pumping it. He moaned loudly, opening his eyes and looking down to see the tendons in her forearms flex and tense with each stroke. Part of him worried someone might walk in, but most of him didn't care. He didn't want her to stop. "Love seeing how hard you are for me" she whispered, her voice low and sultry. She pushed him backwards, walking him over to one of the benches which was set up like a seat. His knees bumped against it and she pushed him down onto it. Sitting like this he felt vulnerable and exposed, gazing up at her, and admiring her body. She was tanned, and looked like a Goddess, even in the unforgiving light of the gym. She stepped forward, her tanned thighs on either side of him, and her arms holding the top of the bench over his shoulders. She lowered herself down, grinding against his cock and he moaned at the contact.

"You like that?" she asked, and Danny nodded. She knew he liked that, he thought. "Want more?" said Amelia, sweetly and he nodded again. "Ask nicely" she added and Danny swallowed, hoping his voice wasn't about to give out on him.

"Please" he said, finally. He wanted her so badly he thought he might be about to explode from the desire. "I love being with guys like you" she said, standing up and hooking her thumbs under the waistband of her tiny shorts. She started to inch them lower, down and over her hips. "Being with someone who reminds me how much stronger I am. It's not the only reason I spend so much time in the gym, but…" she grinned at him, her eyes flashing. "It definitely helps."

She tugged her shorts off, dropping them on the floor, clearly not concerned about anyone walking in. Danny's hands gripped the sides of the chair bench tightly, his knuckles turning white. Amelia stepped forward again, and her pussy was level with his face. He breathed in deeply, the smell making his cock even harder. He could smell how wet she was, how turned on this was making her. Slowly, she lowered herself down, sliding her pussy up and down his cock, teasing and teasing. He bit his lip to keep from letting out a whine as she did. She smirked, and reached down with one hand to stroke his cock again, now wet from her juices.

"I'm going to fuck you" she said, confidently, and Danny knew immediately that she was right. She was definitely going to be the one doing the fucking, he suddenly knew. His cock slid inside her, and he sighed, his mouth falling open at how good it felt. Her pussy was hot and wet, and tight. Somehow it felt muscular, but he didn't even know if that was possible. Still, she felt different to all the other girls he had been with. He reached up and grabbed her arms, feeling how they tensed and moved under his fingers. Her biceps were so big he couldn't wrap his hands around them. She rocked her hips, and the muscle of her ass slid over his thighs as she did, the hardness of her body contrasted against his. He felt her squeezing around his cock, and she reached down with one hand to rub her clit.

"Have you ever fucked a muscle girl like me before?" she asked.

Danny shook his head. "No" he breathed. "Wanted to" he added, not sure where it had come from, but knowing it was true.

Amelia moved her hips faster, and Danny could feel her getting even wetter as she did, her pussy dripping down over his cock, over his hips. He wondered if she was going to leave a puddle of juice on the seat, so wet it was dripping down over his thighs. No wonder he had been able to smell her when she was spotting him the other day, he thought. He wondered if she had been thinking about fucking him like this since the first session they had together. He shivered at the thought, the way she had humiliated him, teased him, reminded him over and over how much stronger she was. He felt his balls tighten at the thought. Her chest was pressed against his, and he could feel how much broader than his it was.

Every part of her body was bigger, stronger, more developed than his, he realized. He felt small next to her, weak, pinned to the seat. He didn't want to move, but he couldn't have if he tried. The idea made his cock pulse, and she grinned at him at she rolled her hips again. "You're not going to cum until I'm finished with you" she said, confidently. She rubbed her clit again, sighing as she did, then biting her lip. He felt her pussy tighten and contract around his cock, and suddenly get even wetter.

She moved faster now, grinding quick and hard against his cock, and he could feel her tighten over and over, as she came again and again on his cock.

"I'm going to…" he began, trying to control himself and gripping even more tightly to her arms.
"Not yet" she said, a glint in her eyes, and he pulled in another deep breath through his nose. Amelia shuddered and came once more, and she looked at him and whispered "now. Come for me now."
Danny felt a shiver run through his body as she spoke, and the orgasm pulsed through him, shooting his load deep inside her as her pussy tightened, milking every last drop of cum out of him. He threw his head back, moaning loudly until finally he was spent.

A few minutes later, Amelia carefully lifted herself off him, his seed dripping out of her and down her thigh. She grabbed the towel he had brought with him for the workout. "You don't mind if I use this, do you?" she asked, as she used it to wipe some of the cum and sweat off herself. "I'll give you something to take home as a souvenir" she smirked, throwing the towel at him. He caught it awkwardly, feeling his cheeks flush once more.

Amelia picked her shorts up off the floor and gracefully shimmied into them, tugging them back over her hips. "Another after hours workout next time?" she asked, and Danny nodded weakly. Maybe he did like the gym after all.

Chapter 1.

Dean checked his phone anxiously, waiting to see if Maria was going to message back before he had to turn on airplane mode. They had been messaging infrequently the last few weeks, and even though he knew he probably didn't need to worry, well. He was worried. He always thought that the two of them were pretty solid, but this trip had dragged on and one, running way way over time. He wouldn't blame her if she was getting frustrated – he was meant to be off for three weeks, max, and somehow that had turned into six months.

The project had been a disaster and Dean was as excited to see the back of it as he was to see her, and see home, again. He missed her, and the daily phone chats were no substitute for having her next to him, he thought. The last few weeks though – something had seemed off. She missed him, she said, but her messages had been coming through irregularly. She had been dropping vague hints about some sort of new hobby she had been occupied with. He had asked questions, of course – he wanted to know what she was up to, and he hated not being around to support her with whatever was getting her so excited. She had been dismissive though, or evasive. He knew it was probably just paranoia, but he couldn't help but worry that her 'new hobby' might be a new guy.

He felt guilty even thinking that. Guilty both because it made him feel like he was being unfair to her – he ought to trust her more than this, right? But also because on some level he couldn't blame her if she had gotten lonely and taken matters into her own hands. Maria had always had a high sex drive – it was one of the things they had in common, which he loved about their union, and he could only imagine how she would be faring after six months with no sex. She must be climbing the walls, he thought. He tried not to ruminate on the thought too much. He didn't need to spend the next eight hours worrying she had been cheating, and he probably didn't need to spend it thinking about having sex with her either. The separation had been rough on him as well, and frankly he was running on a hair trigger – he couldn't remember getting so many unexpected or unwanted hard-ons in years. He hoped whatever she was up to, she could afford to take a few days off once he got home. He had plans that involved getting into bed and not leaving for a while once he finally landed. Dean thought about how good it was going to be to feel her soft hair in his fingers, her smooth skin pressed next to his.

He looked at his phone one last time, the last message had sent her still sitting there unread, and sighed. The intercom dinged through the cabin, reminding everyone to switch their phones off for take-off, and Dean complied, sighing again as he did. He settled back into his seat, resigning himself to a restless few hours, and tried in vain to relax. There wasn't really anything more he could do at this point, he figured, and worrying wasn't going to make the plane arrive any faster. Hopefully she would let him know what the new hobby was once he saw her. He didn't think he could handle another minute of suspense. The plane slowly rumbled underneath him, the noise of it taxiing to the runway blotting out his thoughts momentarily.

Chapter 2.

Dean arrived at the airport feeling tired and too-awake, all at the same time. He had been chugging back the horrible airplane coffee the entire trip, trying to keep himself alert, and instead he thought he might have overshot the mark a little – he was practically vibrating from all the caffeine. He trudged through the arrivals hall, squinting at the signs, trying to figure out where the hell he was meant to pick up his suitcase. He got turned around about three times before he ended up in front of the right glass corridor, which spat him out into a noisy, bustling hub-bub of people. It was sort of overwhelming. Dean blinked for a few moments, looking around to see if he could spot Maria.

Suddenly he spotted her, waving from the very back of the hall. He lugged his suitcase behind him, trying to weave through the crowds. She was dressed weirdly, given the summer heat – wearing a giant oversize sweater and sweatpants. Dean wouldn't normally have noticed what she was wearing after so long apart, more interested in getting her undressed, but usually Maria was a big fan of tiny shorts in summer. This was out of character. He hoped it wasn't a sign that something was wrong. She waved again, more enthusiastically now he was closer, and he pushed the thoughts out of his mind, just happy to be home.

She practically jumped on top of him as soon as he was
close enough, kissing him enthusiastically, and clearly not
caring who was watching. That made Dean relax a little –
whatever was going on, she obviously hadn't gotten bored
of him, or decided she wanted to break up.

"Good to see you too" he laughed, when they pulled apart
a little. He looked at her face – something about it looked
different, although he couldn't place exactly what. Maybe
her jaw looked finer. Had she lost weight? Was her face
thinner? He didn't think she needed to loose any weight,
but he knew better than to ask directly if that was what
had happened.

"Do you need a hand with your suitcase?" she asked with
a grin, and picked it up easily with one hand. Dean tried to
mask his surprise. That thing was heavy. He'd been
hauling it about behind him for fifteen minutes and it felt
like it was about to wrench his shoulder out of its socket.
How the hell had Maria just picked it up like it weighed no
more than a box of cornflakes?

He tried to size up how she looked under the
sweatshirt. What had changed while he was away?

She kept up a happy running commentary as they
walked back to the car, explaining how work had been
going, and asking him questions about the project.
Everything she had obviously been waiting to tell him
came spilling out, and he felt himself relaxing little by
little, relieved that whatever weirdness he thought had
been there must have been all in his mind. The climbed
into the car, which was baking hot from the sun, and he

noticed Maria still wasn't taking off her sweater. He could see beads of sweat collecting around her hairline. "Aren't you boiling in that thing?" he asked, tugging at one of the sleeves.

Maria looked slightly embarrassed, her cheeks heating. "I'll take it off when we get home" she said, sounding awkward. Dean felt like there must be something he was missing. He had thought they seemed to have slotted right back into their old routine, but she seemed weirdly reluctant to take off a sweater… was she going to feel weird about being nude in front of him? Dean's cock gave a twitch at the thought of her naked. He really hoped that wasn't going to be a problem…

"So what's the new hobby?" Dean asked, trying to sound casual.

Maria grinned impishly. "Well…" she began. "It's… I'll show you when we get home" she said, after a pause.

"Can I guess?" Dean asked. "If you're going to show me… is it something you've made? Built?"

"I guess you could say I've built it" said Maria, sounding mysterious. Dean was even more intrigued than before.

The drive went quickly, which was good because between the desire to get Maria home, and ideally naked, and the intense curiosity he felt about whatever her secret new hobby was, Dean felt like he might be about to burst. Maria lifted his suitcase easily out of the trunk when they pulled into the driveway, picking it up in one hand as though it weighed nothing at all. Dean had a sudden moment of panic wondering if maybe it DID weigh nothing. Had he picked up the wrong suitcase? One that looked like his but was entirely empty? But he knew that wasn't right, because he remembered groaning as he hauled it off the conveyer. Maria must just be stronger than he remembered. He was about to open his mouth to say as much when she unlocked the door, stepped inside, and took off the sweater, finally, and his mouth fell open but no words came out.

She smiled shyly at him. "What do you think?" she asked. Now she was wearing just a tank top he could see that she had gotten stronger while he was away – much stronger, from the looks of things. Her arms were thick with muscle, her biceps hard and bulging, and her shoulders were rounded, capped delts popping out of either side of the tank. Dean blinked for a moment, taking it all in.

"Wow" he said, after a moment's pause. "You've been-" he started.

"Going to the gym a bit, yeah" she finished.

"A bit?" said Dean, his voice squeaking slightly. It looked like Maria might have been living at the gym. She was jacked, her entire body transformed into what looked like solid slabs of muscle. She smiled again, her eyes flashing flirtatiously as she did and she cheekily flexed one arm.

"Why'd you keep it a secret?" he asked, suddenly.

Maria smiled, looking slightly shy suddenly. "Well" she began, "I've always thought being really really muscular would be hot – but I didn't know if you'd agree. And I figured… while you were away, I could try it out. Then I started and I didn't want to stop – I just wanted to keep putting on muscle, getting bigger and bigger."

Dean nodded, slowly. "I um, I agree" he said. "That's it's hot" he added, maybe unnecessarily. He assumed the look on his face was conveying how he felt about her new look, but no sense risking it being misinterpreted, he figured.

"Also" added Maria, "I figured I needed something to burn off all the energy while you were away" she explained. "Shut the door, would you?" she asked, gesturing and Dean realized he had left it wide open behind him, too shocked to move. He quickly obeyed and Maria smiled again, then hooked her thumbs under the waistband of her sweatpants, sliding them off her hips, leaving her standing in just a thong and the tank top. Now she was almost naked he could see her thighs and calves were thick, solid muscle too, her ass even rounder and tighter than it had been before. Maria had always been quite fit and toned, but this was different – she looked like some kind of Amazonian warrior, he thought.

He could feel himself getting harder by the second, more aroused by the sight than he would have thought possible. Any fatigue he had had after the flight was melting away, replaced with a heady thrum of arousal pulsing through his veins. "You look incredible" he breathed, finally.

"You like it?" she grinned. "I'm a lot stronger now too" she added.

"I noticed" said Dean, then "the suitcase" he explained, with a wave of his hand.

Maria giggled. "Oh yeah. It's not so heavy for me, I guess."
"Could you lift me?" asked Dean, without really thinking about what he was saying.
Maria looked him up and down, squinting for a second. "I think so" she said, then stepped forward confidently, scooping him up.
Dean let out a squeak of surprise. He hadn't been serious, or at least, he didn't think the answer was going to be yes when he asked the question. He felt surprisingly secure in Maria's arms, although the sensation of being relatively smaller and weaker next to her was new.

"Want me to carry you to the bedroom?" she purred into his ear, and Dean nodded, overwhelmed by the feeling of being picked up like he weighed nothing, and the thoughts about what this might mean for the sex they were undoubtedly going to have next.

Chapter 3.

Maria dropped Dean onto the bed, and stood back so he could admire her new physique. His eyes raked appreciatively up and down her body. "So how long have you been-" he started, then trailed off. "You've gotten so..." he didn't finish the sentence. He didn't really need to.

Maria grinned again. "Since your trip got extended. To be honest-" she paused, looking furtive. "I took a couple of supplements. One of the other girls at the gym recommended them. They, um. Well, they've got one major side effect though."

"Oh?" said Dean. "What's that?"

Maria stripped off her tank top before she answered, revealing her perky breasts, and her nipples, already hard. "My sex drive is kind of through the roof. I've been going nuts waiting for you to get home. I've been getting myself off a couple of times a day, but it just isn't as good as your cock" she finished.

Dean realized he was still sitting in the middle of the bed fully clothed, staring at her. He couldn't help himself: obviously he had always found Maria beautiful, but like this, she was stunning. He could hardly look away. He paused, hands moving to unbutton his jeans and then to tug off his t-shirt. He didn't get undressed with anything like the grace that she did, but it didn't really matter – soon they were both naked on the bed. She climbed onto the bed, crawling up towards him, holding eye contact, a hungry look on her face. Moving closer, she straddled him, her muscular thighs on either side of his hips, sliding her wet pussy against his hard cock. She leaned down, kissing him, and his hands came up to grab onto her, one on her hard bicep, another on her breast, stroking her nipple. She moaned into his mouth and her hips gave another little flick over his cock.

"I want to taste your cock again" she whispered in his ear, the words sending little goosebumps erupting over his arms. She braced herself, lines of hard muscle standing out around her triceps and biceps, and slid down the bed, nosing at his cock, before licking a long stripe up it from the base to the tip and taking it into her mouth. Dean moaned and threw his head back against the pillows, the feeling of her mouth after so long even more incredible than he had remembered. She bobbed her head, slowly at first, then faster, her hand working his shaft as she did, curling her tongue under the ridge at the head of his cock.

"Maria you need to slow down, I'm going to..." he started, panting and out of breath already. She pulled off his cock, looking up at him, her eyes dark with lust under the long lashes. From here he could see how strong her shoulders were, wider than they had been before and flexed casually as she supported herself easily on the heels of her hands. She slid off him, kneeling beside him on the bed and grabbed his hand, guiding it towards her pussy. She was wet under his fingers, juices sliding down over his hand as he rubbed her clit, and she moaned and slid her hips over him, urging him to move faster until he slid his fingers inside her. She was hot and wet and tight, squeezing around them, and he reached down and squeezed the base of his cock, the idea of what she would feel like when he fucked her almost too good to bear.

"Yeah, fuck" she moaned, biting her lip, her head thrown back and her hair cascading down between her shoulder blades. "Don't stop, I'm going to…" as she spoke her hips buckled slightly, her cunt squeezing tight around him, and he could feel a rush of wetness as she came on his hand. He was surprised, but pleasantly – he and Maria had always fucked a lot, but getting her to come could be tricky. Maybe the sex drive boost she mentioned had something to do with this?

She was breathing heavily and he withdrew his fingers, sliding his hand, wet with her juices across her hip and grasping her round ass, pulling her towards him for a kiss. She leaned in, her tongue swiping over his lips, and then tugged at his shoulder. "Want you to fuck me" she explained. "Like this" she added, as she bent over on all fours, arching her back and spreading her legs.

Dean didn't need to be told twice. He moved behind her, running his hands over her ass and admiring how she looked like this, all the planes of muscle in her back laid out for him to see. Looking down the curve of her ass melted into her hamstrings. If you'd asked him yesterday he never would have said he had a muscle fetish, but now he had his bodybuilder girlfriend bent over in front of him like this… it seemed like he might after all. His cock was hard and throbbing, pre-cum leaking from the tip, and he guided it carefully towards her wet and swollen pussy. Her thighs were slick with wetness already, and he moved slowly, teasing her. She let out a high pitched whine as he did.

"Dean" she said, her words sounding desperate. "Babe, I need you to fuck me." He slid his cock fully into her, sighing at the feeling of being buried deep in her tight wet folds, contrasted with the hardness of her tanned body under his hands. Slowly now he began to thrust, focusing on how she felt. Maria had always had a tight little pussy, gripping his cock and milking it when they fucked, but somehow she felt both tighter and wetter now. She shuddered and moaned as he thrust deeply into her, her breath coming in short fast gasps. "Fuck, yeah, faster, you're going to make me-" the sentence was cut off as she thrust back quickly into him, her hips keeping a quick beat as she moaned and shook again, wetness squirting around his cock and dripping onto the covers underneath them. Dean moaned now, the feeling of her tightening and coming on his hard cock overwhelming.

"Don't stop" she said through gritted teeth, the last shudders of the orgasm still rippling through her body, and he kept thrusting, faster and deeper now. She was thrusting back into him, each stroke landing harder and deeper than the last, and Dean squeezed his eyes tightly shut, focusing on the feeling and trying to make it last. He wondered if he might be able to make her come again, but...

"I want to come with you this time" she said, her words breathy. She was moaning with every thrust now, the sound turning Dean on even more than he thought possible. God, he didn't think they had had sex like this since they started dating… maybe not even then. Maria wasn't usually this direct and bossy, and he found he liked it, having her basically ordering him to fuck her. His cock was throbbing now, and he could feel the orgasm building. "Want you to come in me" she gasped, and that was almost enough to set him off by itself, the idea of shooting deep inside her, filling her up with his seed.

"Maria, I'm going to" he started, and she reached down, rubbing her clit as he fucked her. He couldn't get the rest of the words out, fucking her through the orgasm and feeling her tighten around him again, milking the cum out of him. His cock pulsed, pumping his load deep inside her, and it felt like the orgasm went on forever, rippling through his entire body, all of his muscles tensing and sparks erupting behind his eyes. Finally, he pulled out of her, collapsing, sweaty and sated, on the bed next to her. She curled up next to him and rested her head sweetly on his chest. "Love feeling you come inside me" she said, sounding content.

There was a pause, then. "Maybe you can lick me clean later?" she suggested. Dean paused. They hadn't tried that before, but well… if it meant Maria might come like that all over his face… he could definitely be game for something new.

Emily: Muscle Girl Tales III

Chapter 1.

Simon glanced over at Emily again, checking to see if he was imagining things. He only really saw her when they got together for these movie nights – the whole group of them had stayed consistent with them for years, and Emily always made it along, but these days it was more like once every few months. He had never really looked at Emily, or – he had never really looked at Emily like that. He had always seen her as one of the boys, or something like that – he frowned. Was that sexist? He wasn't sure. He had never checked her out, anyway.

Well, he wasn't exactly checking her out now. He was more just… curious. She looked buff. Like she had put on some muscle. She was wearing a white t-shirt, and the sleeves were tight around her biceps. She reached forward to grab the can of soda off the table in front of her, and the muscles through her forearms flexed as she did. He glanced again – the shirt was low-cut, and he could see the line of pecs running down her chest. Simon looked away quickly, in case it seemed like he was staring at her chest. Which he sort of was, he supposed, but not like that.

Had Emily always been this fit? He couldn't remember. The last time they all got together it was winter, so she had probably been wearing a sweater, he reasoned. He looked back at the screen in front of him, not paying attention to the film. He'd watched it a few times before, he knew what was going to happen next. That wasn't really the point of these evenings. They had all studied together, and hung out in college, helping each other cram for exams, and celebrating graduations. Once they had finished college they all made a promise to keep seeing each other regularly. Simon hadn't thought it would last more than a year at most, but five years later and they were still doing this a few times a year. It was fun, everyone just dropped easily back into the roles they'd had when they were younger. They were all approaching 30 now, but sometimes it was fun to act like a 20 year old again, eating junk, and teasing each other, and watching dumb action movies.

Emily was the only girl in the group – so they tended to do what Simon supposed were probably dumb jock things, but she never seemed to mind. Maybe that was why she had started lifting weights? That was a thing jocks did. Well. Simon thought it was – he had never really seen the inside of a gym himself. He was lucky that he stayed pretty trim without much work, but he didn't have any muscle to speak of. Emily's arms looked like they were nearly twice the size of his.

Why was he so obsessed with thinking about it suddenly? He couldn't figure out why it bothered him. It wouldn't be like she was the first one of his friends to suddenly bulk up and get into protein shakes. She was the first girl he had known to do this though. If that was what she had done, of course. Maybe it was a trick of the light. He slid his eyes sideways, trying to be discreet about it. Definitely not a trick of the light – her arms were huge now, thick veins snaking down the outside of them, and even her forearms looked bigger, ropey tendons visible under the skin. What the hell. How had she gotten so big?

Just then Emily looked across and met his eyes. Simon could feel himself turning red. Caught out.
"What are you looking at?" she asked. She'd always been pretty direct – out of all of them, she was often the first to jump in and point out if someone was acting like a jerk.
"Nothing" said Simon, unconvincingly.
Emily raised her eyebrows at this. "You've been staring at me on and off all evening. What's the deal, dude?"

Everyone else started to look around, shifting their attention from the screen to the conversation between Simon and Emily. Simon wanted to sink into the couch, then maybe into the floor underneath it. "What's up?" said Grant, from his left.
Simon sighed. "Um, it's just…" he began. "You're looking really muscular" he said, sounding small.
Emily giggled. "Oh! Yeah, it's this new routine I've been doing." She flexed one of her arms casually, the sleeve of her shirt pulling even tighter around her biceps. "Why were you staring? Trying to see if you could beat me in an arm wrestle?" she winked as she said it.
Simon could feel all the eyes in the room on him now. They knew what that was, and so did he. That was a challenge.

He looked at Emily's arms, sizing them up. They were much bigger than his. There was no way he was going to win this, he knew. "I reckon I could beat you in an arm wrestle" he said out loud, and around them whoops erupted from the rest of the guys. Simon didn't know why he'd said that. He was going to be humiliated, and everyone was going to see it.

Grant was shifting pizza boxes off the table to create a makeshift competition space, and Scott was loudly declaring himself the umpire, on account of having once refereed a wrestling match in college. Emily looked at Simon and smirked. "You sure about this?" she asked. Simon shrugged helplessly. Not really, he thought, but not much I can do now. What was he going to do? Back out? That was maybe the only thing that could be more embarrassing, he thought.

Chapter 2.

Emily's hand was smaller than his, but he could feel how strong it was as they both lined up. He met her eyes as they knelt on either side of the table. Simon couldn't believe how anxious he was about this stupid arm wrestle. That was definitely the feeling gripping him, he decided. He was anxious. He wasn't having any other feelings or reactions to the idea of Emily beating him at arm wrestling, none at all. None that he wanted to think about too hard right now, anyway. He tried to clear his mind. Zen. Something like that. It was hard, surrounded by pizza boxes, but he tried.

Emily's hand was strong and warm in his, and looking across the table his eyes fell on her chest again, pecs and cleavage right in his line of sight. He was fucked, he knew. She was almost certainly stronger than him, and even if she wasn't, he kept getting distracted by the stupidest things – like staring at her body. Above them, Scott was giving a running commentary like he was warming up the crowd at a boxing match. Oh god, please let this end quickly, thought Simon.

"Ok, on three!" said Scott, shaking Simon back to reality. He tried to brace himself, tensing his arm. He suspected it wouldn't make a difference. "One…" Scott started to count, and Emily looked Simon dead in the eye. "Two…" Simon swallowed hard, and Emily smirked, then licked her lips. Simon felt his cock starting to get hard, what was going on, he wondered, why was he… "Three!" yelled Scott, and suddenly Emily's hand was pushing his over towards the table and oh god, he was losing already, and he was losing so badly, he panicked and tried to fight it, his arm tensing and screaming, his muscles burning, but she was so much stronger than him. He tried to pull every ounce of extra energy up from inside himself, drawing on every last reserve of strength he had and grunting as he did. Her hand didn't move, but he stopped her from gaining any ground. They were locked, but she had the power here, and Simon's hand was hovering a few inches above the table. He didn't know how much longer he was going to be able to hold her off, and she was so much stronger than he'd expected. He looked at her arms, seeing the muscles really bulging now they were being put to the test, and swallowed hard. Something about being beaten by her, feeling how easily she could overpower him in the arm wrestle was making his throat dry.

"Sure you could beat me huh?" muttered Emily under her breath and Simon closed his eyes, hoping he might be able to summon up some last burst of strength. He let out a low and guttural groan, but as he did she pushed down with even more force, somehow she had been holding back, and she had reserves where he didn't, pushing his hand down onto the table. Scott held her hand up like she was the victor in a boxing ring, and Simon closed his eyes in shame.

It took about fifteen minutes for the yelling and laughter to die down, and then half the room wanted to grill Emily about what her weightlifting routine was. She laughed and grinned, relishing the attention, and flexing a little for the admiring crowd. Simon hung back, trying to disappear, busying himself in the kitchen. Finally he heard the noise of the movie being put back on, and thought it might be safe to return to the lounge, maybe the worst of the teasing might be over with now. As he turned, Emily entered the kitchen though, and Simon froze. He couldn't work out what was going on – since when had he had a crush on Emily? Or been into muscular women? Or been into Emily specifically when she was this muscular? He couldn't figure out which one it was, but maybe it didn't matter given how his cock kept getting hard every time he thought about how it felt to experience all of her strength overpowering him like that.

"You doing ok?" she asked. He couldn't read her face or tone of voice as she asked. He stood awkwardly in front of Emily, not sure what to do with his hands.

"Yeah, fine" he said, his voice sounding unusually high and fast as he spoke. "Congratulations on your victory, I guess" he added.

Emily smiled, then looked thoughtful. "You seemed pretty interested in my muscles before" she said, her voice even, like she was just commenting on the weather.

Simon nodded, and swallowed. She must be able to tell the effect she was having on him, he knew it. As the thought crossed his mind, her eyes dropped to his crotch, and he felt his cheeks instantly heat in a blaze of colour.

"Really really interested in them, huh?" she said. Emily stepped in closer to Simon, so there was only a few inches between their chests, and now she was so close he could see the muscle through her neck too. Why was he focused on this? He didn't understand. He should be worrying about whatever she was going to say to the rest of the guys, he thought. Instead all he could think about was if the rest of her body was this muscular as well.
"I guess" he said, finally. "You're um. I haven't seen many girls who look like you" he finished, finally.
Emily looked thoughtful, and stepped back. Simon breathed a sigh of relief, but was still confused. What were they doing? It felt like the tension between them was still wound tight. "Did you drive?" she asked, suddenly.
Simon nodded. "Yeah. Why?"
"I caught the subway, but it looks like we're finishing up late. Can you give me a lift home?"
Simon nodded. "Yeah of course." He was pretty sure what she was actually asking, but he wasn't dumb enough to say it out loud and break the spell, he decided.

Chapter 3.

Scott waved from the doorstep, yelling something about a rematch at the next movie night. Simon waved in return and rolled his eyes. Emily walked beside him, and there was still something thoughtful and deliberate in her movements. He unlocked the car and she slid into the passenger seat. "You know the way to my house, right?" she asked.

Simon nodded. "Past the bridge, then a left?"

"That's the one. Unless you want to take a detour."

Huh. That was a lot more direct than Simon had been expecting, but, well. If that was how Emily wanted to play it… Simon was kind of coming off the back of a long dry spell. And whatever it was about Emily that had caught his attention, he would be pleased to figure it out in a bit more detail. "A detour?" he said out loud.

Emily looked at him with innocent eyes. "In case you need to stop for gas maybe. Then it's faster to take the third exit off Brookes."

"Oh, right. No I'm good" said Simon, starting the car and trying to focus on the driving. The last thing he needed to do was ding a lamppost pulling out of the park or something, he'd embarrassed himself enough already this evening. As they pulled onto the main road, he felt Emily's hand reach across and settle on his thigh. He remembered how strong her hands had been in his, and shivered

reflexively at the feeling of her touching him again. He
made a questioning noise, and Emily giggled.

"I was fucking with you, I'm sorry" she said. This was
more like the Emily he knew, he thought. "Honestly, it was
kind of hot seeing you so obsessed with how strong I was"
she continued. Simon nodded, not trusting his voice right
now and feeling his cock growing just from the proximity
of her hand. "Have you always been into muscular
women?" she asked, conversationally, her fingers sliding
back and forth on his thigh.
"I don't know" he said, before he could think of a better
answer. "I um- I didn't know I was? Am?" He paused.
"I'm into you, though" he added.
"Hmmmm" Emily made a noise, as though she was rolling
that piece of information around in her mouth. Her hand
reached further over Simon's lap and her fingers brushed
his cock through his pants. He was properly hard now, his
cock straining against the zipper, and he thought he would
probably need to pull over soon, or at least get off the main
road, because he could hardly focus on talking, let alone
trying to drive in this state. "Do you want to find out?" she
asked, like she was asking if he wanted another piece of
pizza. How was she staying so calm and serene? Simon
could feel sweat beading at his hairline, confused and
aroused by how completely cool and in control she was.

"Yeah" he said, finally. He signalled for the next off
ramp, and headed towards one of the look-outs on the
edge of town.
Emily figured out where they were headed after a few

seconds. "Old lover's lane, huh?" she asked.

"I mean… that's what you mean, right?" Simon asked.

Emily laughed properly now. "Oh my god, I didn't mean to confuse you this much. Yes, that's what I meant. Honestly, it's been fun seeing guys lose their minds over how jacked I am and how turned on that makes them, I figured – I may as well have a bit of fun with it. You remember how buttoned up I was in college, right?"

Simon nodded.

"I'm making up for lost time" said Emily, with a shrug, as though it were as simple as that.

Simon's cock was still hard, and he was pretty sure he wasn't making decisions with any other part of his body, like his brain, right now. Would this make things awkward at the next movie night? He didn't care. He just needed to be able to touch Emily's muscles again.

He pulled into the small and deserted car park after what felt like an eternity, but was probably only a few minutes. It was dark up here, only the lights of the city in the distance. There was a click as Emily unbuttoned her seatbelt and swivelled around to face him. She gripped his cock through his pants properly now, and he moaned at the touch, his hips coming up to meet her hand. He stroked her arms now, touching the swell of her biceps and tracing the line of muscle up to her shoulders. She grinned and grabbed his other hand, placing it on her chest. He stroked the soft curve of her breast where it turned into the hard planes of muscle through her pecs, and shivered.

"Should I take it off?" she asked, unnecessarily, as she tugged at her shirt. She was already lifting it over her head before Simon could reply. In the dim illumination from the far off street lights he could see the contours of her muscles, the ridges of her abs. Her arms were impressive, but now he saw that they weren't the only part of her that was thick with muscle, honed and shaped. In awe, he reached out and ran his fingers down her stomach, over her hard abs, and along the lines that ran diagonally into the waistband of her jeans. Even sitting down like this, it was clear there wasn't any fat on her – she was pure, sleek, powerful muscle. Just then Emily stroked his cock again, harder, and Simon sighed. Taking that as a yes, she flicked open the button on his pants, and unzipped them, pulling his cock out of his boxers and stroking it more firmly now.

"You're so hard for me" she said, her thumb sliding underneath the head of his cock. Simon just nodded. "Can I blow you?" she asked, but she was already leaning forward. Simon moaned and sank back into the seat, her mouth already on his cock. It was hot and wet, her tongue sliding over it, and he could feel his pulse throbbing through his entire body as she did. "Jesus Christ Emily" he muttered. He ran his hands over her back, feeling the slide of her body over his, and over her shoulders, tensed where she was bracing herself against the seat. She hummed around his cock in reply, and dropped one of her hands to play with his balls as she did. Simon shifted slightly, to give her more space and ran his hand further down her back, to stroke the curve of her round, tight ass. She wriggled back against him as he did, and kept moving her head, bobbing up and down on his cock with deliberate, rhythmic strokes.

She felt so good around his cock, her mouth tight and perfect, her bottom lip dragging over the head of his cock slightly with each up-stroke. She pushed her head down even further this time, and he could feel the head of his cock bump up against the back of her throat as she gagged slightly around him, her throat tightening. His cock was slick with spit, and he was torn between closing his eyes to focus on the sensation, and opening them to get a good look at her as she blew him. Half of his mind wandered, wondering if anyone else might come along and see them here like this, but this time of night anyone else here would surely be up to the same thing. He ran his hand back over her shoulder, down her side, and over her breasts, playing with one of her nipples and feeling it harden between his fingers. As he did, she moaned, the feeling of the noise vibrating through him as she did.

"Emily" he whispered, urgently. He could feel himself getting close, which was honestly a lot quicker than he had expected but… the way she looked, and how dirty this felt, the fact they were practically in public… it was a lot, and it was almost overwhelming him. She pulled off his length, licking her lips, which were glossy and swollen in the half-light, her eyes dark with lust. "Do you want to…?" he started, letting her guess the rest of the sentence.
"Want you to come in my mouth" she said, decisively. "I want to taste you." She dropped her head again,

swallowing him down with renewed vigour, her throat working around the head of his cock again, and her strong but soft hands cupping and cradling his balls. He could feel the orgasm starting to wind itself through his body, feel that he was getting closer and closer.

"I'm going to" he began, but couldn't finish the sentence. He started to come, his cock jerking and spurting, as her mouth continued to move over him, but slower now, softer. She was hot and wet around him as the orgasm rolled through his body, and he could feel her swallowing down his load as his balls emptied, draining a thick load of cum into her mouth. Finally, the sparks of the orgasm started to recede, and he drew in a long and shaky breath. Emily sat up, licking her lips, and wiped her hand on the seat of the car. She grinned at him, and Simon smiled back, sure he must have the dopiest look on his face. He felt sort of like she'd sucked out half his brains, he reflected.

Emily looked around the car, until she found her shirt where she'd thrown it in the back seat and shrugged it back on. Simon was sort of disappointed at her covering her muscular physique back up, but also… they probably couldn't drive home like that. "You know the way back to my place?" she asked, and Simon started the car by way of answer.

"Maybe we could think about a little rematch next time" said Emily, thoughtfully, as they pulled out of the car park.

Simon's eyebrows shot up.

"I mean, I think I'd probably win, but you seemed to come out of that ok after all" said Emily, in a teasing tone.

About the author:

Ash is an author who loves reading, writing and thinking about dominant and muscular women, and the men who love them. When she isn't writing steamy tales, she loves to hit up the gym and work on her own toned physique! Follow her author page to be notified every time she publishes a new book.

You might also like:

Candy: Strapped Muscle Babes I

Grant is pretty used to being suavely in control in the office, and when a new receptionist arrives he expects she is going to fall all over him like all the other girls do. Candy is something different though – an impossibly muscular redhead, something about her is utterly poised and in control. She isn't fawning over Grant, and he can't shake the feeling that she's the one who is calling the shots in all of their interactions.

Before long, Grant needs a favour, and Candy is the only one who can help – he's going to lose this contract if he can't get across town in the next 28 minutes. "Follow me" says Candy, crisply walking across the polished concrete in her sky-high heels, and Grant obediently trots behind her. "You'll owe me though" she warns. Grant doesn't know what that means, but he isn't in any position to argue.

Later that night, Candy settles herself down on his sofa and opens up the mysteriously large handbag she usually keeps under her desk. Grant is willing to bend over backwards to keep her happy and thank her for saving the day, but this bodybuilding babe has plans to bend him over in a different direction entirely…